Eve the Inventor

Karen Greenbaum-Maya

BAMBOO
DART
PRESS

LOS ANGELES † NEW YORK † LONDON † MELBOURNE

Eve the Inventor by Karen Greenbaum-Maya

978-1-962316-15-6   Paperback

978-1-962316-16-3   Ebook

First Printing 2025

Layout and design by Mark Givens

Photography by Karen Greenbaum-Maya

For information:

Bamboo Dart Press

chapbooks@bamboodartpress.com

Bamboo Dart Press 056

www.pelekinesis.com

www.bamboodartpress.com

SHRIMPER
www.shrimperrecords.com

Ring the bells that still can ring
Forget your perfect offering
There is a crack in everything
That's how the light gets in.
— Leonard Cohen, *Selected Poems, 1956-1968*

Advance Praise for *Eve the Inventor*

When Eve bites into the apple, she invents Time. In the small space of 18 poems, Greenbaum-Maya transverses that time using a cast of heroes: her grandfather the undercover Nazi hunter, her dance teacher Irene Serata, Van Gogh, her classmate the math genius, Fred Astaire and Ginger Rogers, Rembrandt, Einstein (and a mathematical explanation of why he stopped wearing socks). The souls in these pages all embellished this earth with art, music, science, or dance. The author's insights into culture and cultural history are rich and surprising, and often humorous. But she is not naïve. Even in the shadow of war and antisemitism, she manages to build a world where we can believe, once more, that it might all be worth saving. She reminds us that this world, however imperfect, is what we have, that it is rich and worthy—that we each have it in us to make it rich and worthy—and that at least while we are alive, there is *no way to leave.*

    --Donna Spruijt-Metz, author of *Dear Ghost,* (winner, Harbor Review's Editor Prize)

A range of diverse and eccentric voices and characters populate the bizarre world, theatre, stage of Karen Greenbaum-Maya's prose poetry collection. The prose poem is the perfect vehicle for Greenbaum-Maya's sharp and experimental work to shine light on an absurd age. I hope everyone enjoys this memorable, vibrant collection!

    -Jose Hernandez Diaz, Benjamin Saltman Poetry Award 2023 Winner

Karen Greenbaum-Maya's wonderful, slender *Eve the Inventor* demonstrates how a handful of pages can become a multitude in the right hands—a universe populated not just by the Biblical Eve and her serpent but also by George Clooney, Buster Keaton, Rachel Maddow, the fictional Deanna Troi, and more, all mingling with one another and the speaker's relatives, friends, and lost loves, dancing, writing poetry, putting on socks, hunting Nazis. These busy worlds are often dangerous, and they're always fascinating.

   -**David Ebenbach**, author of *What's Left to Us by Evening*

Eve the Inventor, Karen Greenbaum-Maya's new chapbook, mixes elements of the memoir from her previous collection, and combines them with ekphrasis, and touches on a multitude of themes ranging from the detached "care" of the American healthcare system, to what it means to exist is a post-Covid, post-truth America, to gender roles, to the male gaze, to *Star Trek*; and in the specific case of those last three, she does so in the space of a single poem. And throughout the entire collection, Greenbaum-Maya's honesty and insight, always tempered with her specific brand of humor, remain on full display. There aren't enough good things to say about this book, I love everything about it.

   - **Tim Hatch**, author of *Wild Embrace*

Contents

Eve the Inventor

When Eve bites into the apple, she invents Time. She crunches her bite, tastes the juice released from the crushed chambers. She swallows. Now it is Gone. Now there is a Now, becoming Then. Now the bite of apple starts to enter the past, The next bite is a little less crisp. Grasses bend in the new little wind, and the sun starts to drift to the horizon. Eve discovers her apple's green-woody stem that doesn't even know its useful life is over. Birds sing for the first time when their song begins and ends. The serpent is astonished to feel the desire to shed his skin. And Eve has not yet discovered that no good deed goes unpunished.

Young Mustard

The children in the stories I read were safe from going home. By the time I arrived at the new mustard, the air was cooling down. No warmth from the earth. A chilly place but hidden. I'd head there after school. The stories said I was supposed to be able to see out, like a tiger in the grass. Even in those dry times, green shot up after spring rain. Three, four days, so quick. Mustard shot four feet tall, tall enough for me to disappear when I sat down. There were vacant lots then. Houses being built out past ours. We were supposed to keep out, but those beams insisted. I'd heel-and-toe along the 4x4s. Beyond them, before them, the vacant lots filled in with mustard, unintended, undemanded. Wait past a week and it would start to bloom, tough, pungent as shoes worn past their span, that full drift of yellow or purple and white. The three-day window: green, tender enough to crush, juicy stems that stained knees, can't be washed out, tsks of disgust, commands not to go there. I always went there. Green fresh as cracks in the air.

My Grandfather the Lawyer Is Found to be an Undercover Nazi Hunter

I see you've found me out. From a book, of course. I knew you would be a reader. I saw how your Russian-green eyes held mine, even at ten months. And what I did, was the right thing to do. We knew already, even in 1934, what those bastards meant.

Don't think *Chinatown*. Think Eliot Ness, snap-brim fedoras, Fred Astaire suits with high waists, eased through the hips, loose in the thighs. Family photo: Weber and Fields, hottest team in vaudeville, my uncle and his partner, first to ask why the chicken crossed the road. Your great-grandmother, face like a cameo. Your grandmother, never at home in her chic hat, silk stockings sagging, looking like she'd fall over just standing there. Your father, my son, already deaf from meningitis, and your aunt, loveliest three-year-old that ever lived, except you. And she died her next year, dancing in that damned grass skirt in front of the electric heater. She burned to death because your grandmother didn't know how fire worked, fanned the flames instead of smothering them. She could never atone for that, could she? So she kept smothering, and craving oxygen, all the days of her life.

I was hot-shot City Attorney, not bad for a Jewish boy, son of a Russian tailor. I had to wait five years until USC's quota gave me a shot at law school. No wonder David Lewis sounded me out. He saw I burned for more. He put me right at the center, and I stitched together the agents' reports. But he never asked me to infiltrate the brown shirt meetings. I had a family, your deaf father, your crazed grandmother. By then I didn't have my daughter. Your grandmother was just another good reason not to be at home. Sure, there was another woman. Didn't I look like a heel—perfect cover when I stayed late at the office. I found out about the German agents who approached the tech crews at Metro-Goldwyn-Mayer, I took reports from the mother and daughter who were sent to the parties at the beer gardens. They told me all about the home-grown Fascists who weren't even Germans, the sweaty guys in short-sleeved shirts with crummy ties, suits that rode up behind the shoulders, the ones flashing their Colts, trying to look like they were important.

But I was the one sent to meet the Germans with Kultur, the guests of honor at the embassy receptions, string trios playing Beethoven in the background. Jewish violinist, Jewish pianist, Jew on the cello. *Cosmopolitan*, we got called. It meant, we knew about something larger than our own lives. Think I didn't see the cultural attaché flare his nostrils, sniffing for the smell that wasn't there? Think I didn't see the envoy in his European trousers, wiping his hand after clasping mine? Think again. I belonged though I did not pass. My white tie was correct, my shoes were perfect.

Stradivarius

In the Good Old Summertime is a movie that really doesn't give a damn, much ado about not much, what with Uncle Otto the music store owner possessing a Stradivarius that he can't play, what with Judy's anachronistic tight red dress that zips up the back. Set in winter, for pity's sake, maybe to milk Christmas schlock. Van, the romantic lead, is tall and blond, and his chest strains at his shirt. He's a big ol' guitar that anyone can strum. He and Judy Garland are busily enacting their meet cute cliché, conventional sparks flying with nothing at stake, slapping the audience around with their passionless energy, beats predictable as a soap. But how did Buster Keaton end up there? Judy cannot see that he is the real deal, she cannot see the spring of his sharp frame, his taut waist, his eyes and nose so full of heart that they are almost too big for his face. Certainly too big for this studio movie. His cheekbones are eloquent as Lincoln. Buster is Abe Lincoln. And Van is no Jimmy Stewart.

The rest of the cast work at pretending. Buster alone is alive, a silky black satin ribbon binding and twining among the Technicolor polyester costumes. When he dances with Judy, he moves her around the floor with painful awe, as though she might somehow crumble. We know he hangs up that one good black suit in his rooming house closet at night, carefully. When he pratfalls flat out onto Uncle Otto's plot point Strad, his horror hits us in the gut. It is a counterfeit world, but his purity gleams.

Trout Fishing in America

At that time I thought what Trout Fishing In America was calling poetry was posturing, strutting smug, smoking dope and seducing doe-eyed flower children. At that time I thought he was faking a world with epiphanies every seven minutes, where he wandered as a seer not bound by making a living or even getting grades, where he needed no future because he pretended to live in the eternal now and somehow he got away with it. At that time the world or someone provided for him although he wrote stuff like I wrote at that time, and no one told him he needed to have something to say and no one told him, well how do you expect to sound if you get up and read your poem after you've read from Rilke or anyone else, really, at that time? He was so promising at that time that Ferlinghetti gave him the nod at that time and told him he was *un beau naïf* and I guess one thing that makes you a naïf is being in your 30s, maybe the age of Jesus.

At that time Ferlinghetti said he'd hoped Trout Fishing would mature out of naïveté and become, you know, a writer, but Trout Fishing never did, just despaired and finally emptied his head clean out with a bfg and by the time he was found a month later he had become Lord of the Flies, which is to say trout bait. Turns out he was never in the world enough to leave it. You can't say he failed to choose a path in life, failed to make the sacrifice of choosing because by that time it was too late to choose. Richard Brautigan, *Bräutigam* the unconsummated bridegroom, at last consumed.

All I Can Be

Avner, Avner, I failed at becoming you, the way a gas giant planet falls short of becoming a star. You, two years ahead in high school, floating into Harvard, graduating on time, knocking back your doctorate in math in two years, on my favorite topic, number theory. Incantations on the deep nature of 3 and 9 and ONE the mystical unity, the identity of us all. You, publishing papers for other adepts on hermitian symmetric domains and toroidal compactifications. Me, fighting an earworm of Herman's Hermits, puzzled by my college roommate's asymmetrical breasts, figuring out that Shakespeare was really good. You, advancing gallantly through tenure and colleagues, partnering with other math breathers to popularize differential geometry theory and open self-adjoint homogeneous cones. Me, always gauche, heaving to get some air, closed off, at best adjunct, never ever homogeneous, always conehead and alien. You are the keynote speaker at national conferences. I take photos of potatoes. You progress stately up a steady slope. And I've changed direction more times in three years than you in thirty. How's that for numbers? I'm still scrabbling around for identity. Still blowing, hard. Still sitting too much. Still wishing, Avner. Oh, Avner.

Deanna Troi Watches Rachel Maddow

She thought it was bad aboard the Enterprise-D, all those dutiful hyper-conscientious people trying to control their ungenerous thoughts. It's a bitch, always feeling responsible. You have to keep up with every single thing that's going on in the world. Rachel's signature black suit is as good as a uniform. Still, these days Deanna can't stand to know all the crazy stuff. QAnon addicts who won't get vaccines, who attack other people and think they're the victims. Do they have any idea what it's like, when she channels how they feel and the pain they're causing, simultaneously? She wants to tell them that she can't escape, that she always receives both their anger and their shame. And managing all that tension, on the restrictive diet she has to follow. Can't even indulge now and then—a dish of chocolate ice cream shows up like a baby bump. How people would talk. Riker talks a good game, but never ever gets to the point, if you know what I mean. Their anniversary is coming up, and the whole silly crew is going to be warm and supportive and sly, hinting at Ro-Mance. She'll fake it all day long, and no one will have a clue. And walking around in the catsuit? She doesn't get anything like the credit that people give when they drool over Seven of Nine. That outfit! Takes two hours and four assistants to insert the Borg-Girl into it. Deanna is certain that silicone lube is involved somewhere. She just pulls up the catsuit like tights. Doesn't even lift and separate, just flattens. And no underwear of any kind, honey, because the damned thing is a showcase for VPL. How does Rachel never give up? How can she bear to stay tuned in? None of the off-ship people Deanna calls friends want to hear one word about burnout. Thanks to warp speeds, faster than light, she can never get hold of them anyway. At least, that's what they say, that by the time she reaches them, her troubles are so last year. She ought to pay better attention to Rachel's reports, she knows this, but by the time the Enterprise returns to Earth, the news will be old. It won't matter any more.

Sad Clown

Frank Sinatra painted only sad clowns, but no one wanted them. Problem-solver, he donated a five-story wing to the Desert Hospital in Palm Springs. Quid pro quo: *If you accept my paintings, I'll donate walls to hang them.* How bad the admins must have wanted the money! Paintings of clowns lined the lobby, clowns shoulder to shoulder, as you entered or escaped. Broad color blocks crude as a stroke of a paint roller. Grimacing faces under the grease-painted frowns, and burned-out eyes, flat and dead. Eyeholes. Kind of like late-period Frank himself. The sharp-shouldered guy with his doll, the hard-drinking journalist whose comrade became the Manchurian candidate—that guy had gone squat, had turned into a toad.

Every time I left the psych unit, I passed those clowns. The lobby was an indoor short-cut I used to cut down time outside in the late afternoon heat. Frank was still at the easel on his mansion's air-conditioned patio, painting clown after clown from clown paintings he'd seen. The hospital squeezed in a new canvas every few weeks. Weary Willies with round-the-clock 5 o'clock shadows. Perfunctory paper flowers on pipe-cleaner stems sticking out of hats that could not possibly stay on anyone's head. And flat, so flat. His mind must have been elsewhere. As flat as I landed, the time

I crossed paths with the paraplegic in a wheelchair, the halo screwed into his skull to keep his cracked vertebrae from slicing his spinal cord entirely. *You were lucky*, I said. And the guy with the halo looked at my two feet, both in my mouth, and he just kept on looking as I escaped into the heat, Frank in my head singing "Send in the Clowns."

I Learn Gratefully Not to Applaud
Between Movements at Concerts

--with apologies to Leigh Hunt's "Jenny Kissed Me"

Robert Mann, of Julliard,
legendary violin,
raised his finger to his lips,
slowly shook his head, to shush me.

I was gauche, barbarian—
with a flick he could have crushed me.
He, who lightning could have hurled,
saw I sought a better world.
Down the tubes he could have flushed me—
  Robert shook his head, and shushed me.

Say I have no use for rules—
say Fame stumbled, should she brush me—
say that Fortune smiles on fools—!
but say as well, that Robert shushed me.

Carefree

It's always Fred who starts things off, slim tails wafting around his springy frame. Rising weightless as a marionette. He lives by his taps and his wits, sussing out the situation, never down for long, ready and steady. Narrow shoulders, but so what? Too fast to follow, he fires off a riff of easy hands and dazzling black shoes. He rented the tails, but they look bespoke. Might be his costume from the show, the last outfit left after he pawned all the rest to pay a gambling debt. Even as a master thief, because what other kind, he has a code of honor. The primo ballerino of the troupe that can't point their toes. A tap-dancing psychiatrist, bouncing off the walls of his New York office. He's a trickster, clever as Odysseus, master of the double meaning. Loves a prank, turning the tables: the hero as goofball.

Fred might be a swell or a hoofer, but Ginger's always a prole, the working girl who knows the real price of a pair of silk stockings. And a girl's reputation. She's not wealthy, yet her ambitions contrive her a new outfit on every hour. When Fred sees Ginger, he falls for her, just like that. But not Ginger. She's cagy. He has to win her, entrance her, romance her, dance her.

Now it's time for the plot twist. Someone has to interfere. It's Fred's roommate. From college. His henpecked seducer of a producer. Fred's partner George Murphy, who was no Gene Kelly. A dress designer with a Romance accent. *It seems now the rooster is pecking on the other foot, eh my brave?*

Ginger shows her legs right about here, and who can blame her. She is required. Really, check the contract. She rides a bike in white white short shorts, and Fred runs his Schwinn right off the road. Her subdued black dress billows like silk smoke up her white thighs. Her resort outfit features a safari jacket, open over khaki shorts.

Fred cuts a silhouette of a dancing couple, stations it on a Victrola because it's that kind of hotel room, sets a spotlight to show a swoop of a shadow. No one will suspect. Ginger and Fred sneak out to join the big production number: everyone dances the Vittelone, Busby Berkeley's regimented creation. Girls like goddesses out of Egypt, boys sleek as matadors. For the duration, you too are on top, in the know, part of the dance the moment demands.

By the end of the Thirties we're back in the States, and the movies get downright bitter. One more for my baby, and one more for the road, and even war hero Fred goes ballistic and throws that premium whisky right through the mirror. Never gonna dance, never gonna dance no more. We're on the rooftop looking over the edge, but let's not end it all just yet. Let's face the music and dance. They walk offstage, sadder, wiser, earthbound, reconciled to trying again, one more time. They are tired. Just tired.

Seems the war triumphed over the mid-Thirties movies, the ones people mock as confections, cream puffs, lighter-than-air, but those people miss the daring of toying with gravity. More than once, Fred dances across a ceiling, stuffs gravity in his pocket while he sticks the landing on a backflip or pulls off a chest-high standing jump. A flash of triple pirouette *grand battement tendu en l'aire* just for the hell of it, all the time in the world. They dance, and we are there to see it. At first you think *weightless*, but that's senseless, meaningless as a dead leaf. By the end each has lit on the ground among the rest of us, at last able to lie in each other's arms, the hang of the swing of their earthly weight against the other's wakened steadying arm. She fills his hands, and though she is slight as a handful of whipped cream, alights light as a butterfly on a scale, she has become real enough that he must exert something to keep her from dropping into the earth. You can see his hands start to hold her as though his arm is remembering its name, and she lies in his arms as though she has awoken there, and haven't we all, astonished to find ourselves made real. Ready at last to walk off the dance floor, sit down somewhere, speak without words.

Miss Irene

serene Miss Irene Serata
ballet teacher to little girls
    in their unearned tutus

I hated *ronde de jambe*
felt like I was stirring cement with my foot
    I knew they were probably good for me

her dark eyes with clean black outlines
the smooth pale layer painted on her skin
a gauzy pastel scarf tying her curly hair off her face

years later I realized she'd worn stage make-up
Now the scarf veiled her throat
how did she keep the liner from running

The day she stopped dressing for class
    stopped doing barre with us
    (so she would always be ready
    to take her place among the corps)

the day she asked someone else
to demonstrate *sauté* with *double entrechats*
and *tours jèté*

Einstein's Socks

…were not there. He stopped wearing them when he stopped teaching high school kids, before he wrote the wild paper that got him the begrudged doctorate, before he was Herr Doktor Einstein, before he turned 26. Wore high boots to hide his ankles. Loved getting away with the flout. Imagine Einstein teaching geometry and trigonometry, never thinking of asking the kids to show their work. Remember why the Technical Institute held off granting his doctorate? There was nothing wrong with his work. Merely that he had efficiently offended all the proud physics profs, innocently dominating their classes, asking why they hadn't read Lorenz's latest paper or understood the implications of Michelson's measurements of the speed of light, why they hadn't applied the findings to their own stalled projects.

Always, he thought past the box. Proud to ignore the pointless. He cultivated his little ways until no one even expected him to take the time to conform. Saving seconds and minutes, sharp-eyed as any Swiss banker, secreting time away for those insistent daydreams, like music in no one's key.

Princeton let him reset his world to its beginning. Princeton was never as cold as Switzerland, certainly never as cold as Germany, Besides, he simply never got cold feet. Therefore, the solution: if he needed 42 seconds to work socks over his feet; another 74 seconds to stretch suspenders over his calves and wrangle the tops through the grips, then, 34 seconds more to divest himself at night, all that time might be freed. And he would need longer still if his extravagant big toe had poked through the sock, as it did at least once a week. Toe readers tell us, *A sign of creativity! someone who's thinking outside the toe box!* A minimum of 150 seconds a day, an hour and a half a month, eighteen hours a year. Why squander this time relieving the pressures imposed on his feet? Add sock-time to the time he did not spend combing his moustache or taming his hair, at least five minutes, and you can find more than six days, a week's holiday every year. Time to be less interrupted. Time he could let his focus float out to *infinite.* Time to watch his thought experiments unfurl, to listen to the inner music unfolding, sometimes inevitable as Mozart or Bach, never as personal as Beethoven.

The music of his epoch was already going atonal, Schönberg over Schubert. It was clever music but imprisoning, denying the body's satisfaction, denying the deep physical relief that comes with returning to the key, all the threads showing their flowing meaning. Not merely pinpoints or single chords, but shapes brocaded into the fabric of space-time. He eavesdropped on the vibrations, on their overtones, until the variations revealed the one great theme, an unseen sound too bright to view directly, the shining silence of the music playing him.

Man of My Dreams

Can you believe George Clooney and his new book of poetry? Not only did he get paid a billion dollars for his tequila company—not only is he a compelling actor—not only is he the man I don't know whom I most need to see naked—but he can write. Introspective, fresh imagery, intriguing language. And so vulnerable. Who knew he was an introvert?

I want to go buy his book. Judith is ready before I am. I can't find my pants. When I do, they are covered in cat hair. Judith has her pants. She has also published another full-length collection and George recognizes her. *Judith Terzi? You came to my signing? I'm so honored! Let's swap books!* I give up on my pants. I rummage through a hedge of brown paper wrappers for a copy of George's book. Have they all sold? I saw hundreds a few minutes ago. No, there is one last copy of *I'm Just Like You, Only Cooler*. George gives me a tender smile. *We're more alike than you might think*, he murmurs. My eyes spring wide, my words slam shut. I can only sputter and stammer. *Shut up*, Judith hisses, *take the damned compliment.*

Butter-Cake

My friend who was an uncle to me gave me the recipe fifty years back, the recipe he'd recorded from his grandmother, father's mother, not the side of his poisonous mother, but of his gentle and feckless father. He recorded it in his own Labanotation, he charted her moves and Russian-inflected words, he observed. She was the star, he was her biggest fan.

A recipe for people who can't get it right. *Use all the flour. Keep the dough moist. Heat half the milk to boiling, stir in the cold half. Mix thoroughly. Don't touch with your hands! Let it rest. Work fast!* A soft rich dough. Full of oil and sugar, butter and eggs, a pint of milk and two pounds of flour to hold it all together. *Putterküchen.* A preposterously tender dough. Must have used a winter's worth of butter. *That is what the name means, isn't it?* I asked. *Not 'butter,' 'putter,'* he replied. But what else could *putter* have been? And what a silly contradictory dough, raised but not kneaded, each folded circle getting a good quarter-cup of cinnamon-sugar not quite contained by the intricate folds. Another three cups of sugar, third of a cup of cinnamon, just enough water to turn the mix into wet sand, spilling from the slack dough. Extravagant to use so much when you know it will go to waste. And that baking pan was a horror to clean. I had no non-stick pan, too expensive. All my pans were hand-me-downs. I soaked that one for a week before I gave up, threw it away.

She was a witch. Not one who ate children who approached her house of butter-cake, but one who foretold the future. Knew without trying, spoke without knowing. *Don't marry this girl, you'll both regret it.* What did that marriage last, three months? What else did she know? Who knew?. It was the word of the bubbe, hallowed be her name, sanctified be her acts. She was a Jewish grandmother. Was she proud of him, or did she want to flatten his pride? He wrote down every word, admonitions and all.

She was very fat – at least 400 pounds. I try to imagine this. I fail. *But firm. She modeled corsets for catalogs. My grandfather was crazy about her.* Now I see her, a butter mountain, spilling out of the corset the way the cinnamon sugar spilled out of those fussy pastries. Like him I made the recipe just once.

Rembrandt at Fifty

When you look, you see:
he has already sized you up.
Both of you are fifty.
He plays down the all-seeing eyes
peering from his famous shadows.
The arms of his chair give him a throne,
the left hand easy and magisterial,
deploying a paintbrush, or a walking stick,
something with a point
suitable for pointing out.

Those rich fabrics we've seen before.
Perhaps they misdirect us
so we don't read the bulk of his chest
as a maternal swell of bosom,
cinched, but not by the nonchalant sag
of the crimson sash
that brings out the same tone
in his drink-mottled cheeks, his winter-bitten lips,
in the whiskey nose that may be no such thing.

His head covering evades the eye.
The deep brown velvet
isn't easy to distinguish
against the darkness that surrounds him.
That hat makes a hole in the darkness,
shadows those unhesitating eyes.
How could he bear to look and paint
when he beheld himself like this?

Roberta In Winter

Roberta kept making us cards.
They'd permitted her to bring her stamps, her inks,
colored pencils, the embellishments and glue,
all her cardstock, even her scissors.
Here, she was safe at last from the dangers,
from the constant intruders.
Lewy Body dementia had given her comrades:
the watchful ape, the sarcastic little gnome, the two-headed deer,
all more comforting than we could be, now.

1. Happy Winter

Happy Winter slid out of the envelope postmarked TX,
a slip of paper stamped with a snowman.
Happy Winter
    for Persephone, who nibbled just six seeds
Happy Winter   *Let's Celebrate*
on pomegranate cardstock,
one old Jewish lady sending another
a sketchy little owl in a Santa hat,
its stamp unevenly loaded
from a drying ink pad.
Someone at the home must have told her
It's Merry Christmas in America.

That owl was disappearing right into the cardstock
so she gave it all she had.
She tendered orange to the talons,
darker red to the velvet elf hat. With silver
she stroked that faint owl,
scribbled silver on the wings and breast,
scribbled over the round flat eyes.

2. Happy Easter

The woman who'd kept kosher pasted bunnies
onto cardstock pre-printed with eggs.
She seamed the eggs
with All-American baseball stitches.
Faint among the bunnies,
a glimmer of tulle skirt
     yellow curls   frilly wings
     jewel-set crown
     an armful of roses, precise with thorns.

Roberta's dull green pencil informs me:
     those rosy lips and cheeks
     are the Art Fairy, shining through,
     bestowing her gifts
     Once Roberta danced the Rose Adagio.
     Once again she is the Sleeping Beauty.

3. Happy Anniversary

Roberta sent us one last anniversary card.
Her vision granted nothing extra.
She chose for the outer layer a coral cardboard,
yellow tissue for the inner chamber,
but her fingers could no longer make the two papers fold
into each other's embrace.
Liner and cover came unjoined
though she had glued the card shut.

As a giant in a fairy tale,
my outsized eye peers into the housing
at the fortune-cookie message,
caught in lavish glue

> *Believe*
> *Be happy*
> *Love your dream*

Diagnosis as Opera

Note: This work is rarely performed, being overly long and tricky to cast. Prednisone cuts the top off your vocal range. Besides, who wants that old trope of the soprano singing at full volume with pure intonation up to the moment when she dies?

We open on a frenzied party scene. The guests are more colonizer than friend. Our hostess flits and flirts from one group to another. She is dazzling, witty, and yet...and yet there is something forced about her. She turns away for a moment, panting. What. O what. A soulful tenor hastens to her. Would she like him to fetch her maid? She did not expect concern.

The maid takes her to the hospital, to get the diagnosis. Our soprano permits the bone marrow aspiration. We hear the crunch, a Bernstein clatter of percussion, as the metal tube punches into her breastbone. She squeezes the nurse's mezzo hand until the nurse too is bruised.

The physician, a bass, sings a jocular patter aria. He lists all the diagnoses he has ruled out. So pleased with his cleverness. The closing line to each stanza is, *But at least it's not leukemia!* He shows her the slide under the microscope. The slide is projected at the back of the stage. Its pattern, sprinklings of red and purple on mostly filmy white, will be repeated in her next costume change. *Count them*, he commands, and she echoes him as the percussionist gives the beats, *only twelve. There should be one – two – four! A hundred times more!* the physician proclaims, and the projection shows a gorgeous brocade rich with violet knots, a fabric that could stand up on its own. Now a trio featuring our soprano and the physician. He coaches her on pronouncing her rare diagnosis. ImMUno-PAthic THROMbo-CYto-PEneeYA purPUR-ahh. The nurse carries the inner voices. Our soprano warbles, *How can I be diagnosed with what I've never heard of?!* The nurse provides counterpoint: *Why not? Why not? Why not?* Comic relief here in the nurse's exaggerated yelps. Soprano and nurse sing a bittersweet duet that shows how the nurse, though kind, is just doing her job, thinking about what she'll be doing once her shift is over. The soprano will not get time off.

Van Gogh's "Still Life with Anemones"; "Room at Arles"

Now tendrils writhe up from the canvas, spill
across the yellow frame in arsenic green,
his telltale color for what wants to fill

and crowd him out until there's only vines
that halt his brush, then overrun his face.
Too late, now, for the vase's heavy line.

Bed washstand chair: the doctor's house at Arles.
There is no way to walk across the room.
Each shabby piece has warped this smallest world.

His eye advises him not to assume,
not to rely on any point of view.
The chair, the bed, the window do not dream

the same great yellow field to hold them all,
and where they don't agree, the air bleeds out.
He cannot step across. The floorboards fail

to guide him where he never can arrive.
There is no place to live, no way to leave.

Acknowledgments

I thank the editors of these publications where some poems first appeared in similar form.

B O D Y: Sad Clown

Mobius: a journal of social change: She Discovers Her Grandfather the Republican Lawyer Was an Undercover Nazi Hunter

MacQueen's Quinterly: Miss Irene

Offcourse: Eve the Inventor

Psychic Meatloaf: 'Still Life with Anemones,' 'Room at Arles'

Rappahannock Review: Einstein's Socks

Riddled with Arrows: Butter-Cake

Schuylkill Valley Journal Online: At that time; Carefree

About the Author

Karen Greenbaum-Maya is a retired clinical psychologist, former German major and restaurant reviewer, and a three-time Pushcart and Best of the Net nominee. Her work in fairy tales and dream interpretation and her obsession with Kafka and flirtation with Buber have led her inevitably to prose poems. Her poems have received Special Merit and Honorable Mention in the Muriel Craft Bailey Memorial contest from Marge Piercy and from B.F. Fairchild. Her work has appeared in journals including *Comstock Poetry Review, B O D Y, Rappahannock Poetry Review, CHEST,* and *Spillway*. Kattywompus Press publishes her chapbooks *Burrowing Song, Eggs Satori,* and, *Kafka's Cat*. Kelsay Books publishes *The Book of Knots and their Untying.* Bamboo Dart Press publishes *The Beautiful Leaves*, a collection of poetry about her late husband's diagnosis, illness and death, and her grief. She co-curates Fourth Saturdays, a long-running poetry series in Claremont, California. Her first complete sentence was, "Look at the moon!"

112 N. Harvard Ave. #65
Claremont, CA 91711

chapbooks@bamboodartpress.com

www.bamboodartpress.com